Disney · PIXAR

Cars

ON THE ROAD

A Random House PICTUREBACK® Book

Random House 🏠 New York

rhcbooks.com
ISBN 978-0-7364-4346-3 (trade)

Printed in the United States of America
10 9 8 7 6 5 4 3 2 1

DINO PARK

Lightning McQueen and his best buddy, Mater, were on a cross-country road trip. There were all sorts of things to see. They hadn't gone too far, when suddenly—

"Whoa, whoa, whoa!" Mater shouted. A huge dinosaur car loomed over them! As they drove closer, they saw that it was just a dinosaur car sculpture at the entrance of a dino park.

"I love these!" said Lightning. "Let's go see!"

Mater wasn't too interested. "I don't know much about these dino things," he said.

"Well, that's all about to change," said Lightning. He began spouting off dino facts as they made their way through the museum.

Their tour guide pointed at a huge dinosaur car skeleton and said, "This specimen, 536-M, who we affectionately refer to as Mimi, is the most complete skeletal example of a compact theropod. . . ."

The more that Mater listened, the sleepier he got. Soon he drifted off. When he opened his eyes, he was in a strange land full of palm trees and volcanoes. He also looked different—he had become Cave Mater!

"Lightning!" Cave Mater exclaimed. His friend looked like a cave car, too!

Suddenly, a Tyranamissiasaurus rex appeared and clamped down on Lightning!

"Hey, that's sharp!" Cave Lightning shouted.

With a mighty grunt, Cave Mater swung his prehistoric tow hook at the predator and yelled, "Spit him out, you overgrown varmint!"

The dino car roared and dropped Cave Lightning onto the ground.

"Uh-oh," Cave Mater said as the Tyrana rex began to chase him and Cave Lightning.

Just then, an even larger dino car appeared and grabbed the Tyrana rex in its mouth!

"Spinocrankshaftorex—the largest and fiercest of the . . .
GAHHHH!" yelled Lightning.

He and Cave Mater sped away as the two dino cars battled.
But the Tyrana rex grabbed Lightning in its mouth again just
as the two terrible predators tumbled over the edge of a cliff.
They pulled Cave Lightning with them! Cave Mater lassoed his
tow hook around Lightning and tried to pull him free.

"I'll save ya, buddy. . . ."

Mater screamed. His eyes snapped open. He was back inside the museum. "Whew, that was somethin'!" Mater said.

The two friends decided it was time to get back on the road. As they left the dino park, Mater bumped into a Tyrana rex statue. He looked up and saw giant jaws bearing down on him.

"AHHHHHHHH!" Mater screamed, zooming away.

"Wait up, buddy!" Lightning yelled.

SALT FEVER

Lightning and Mater were having the time of their lives on their road trip. They sang songs as they drove along. Soon they noticed that they weren't on any kind of road anymore. They were driving on salt flats.

"Whoa! Land speed racers!" said Lightning as he and Mater entered a camp full of sleek cars.

They watched a long-nosed car with fins being pushed out onto the salt flats.

"Watch out for the Speed Demon!" a crew car said.

"Speed Demon?" Mater asked.

Lightning told Mater that these cars were all about pure speed. Mater liked the sound of that. A utility truck named Noriyuki invited Mater to join his land speed racing team.

"Abso-fantasti-lutely!" exclaimed Mater. He followed Noriyuki into his tent for some upgrades.

BASH! SMASH! CRASH!

The tent opened and the all-new Super Speed Mater rolled out.

A push car moved Mater into position and said,
"Watch out for the Speed Demon!"

"A hundred and seventy-five miles per hour!" said a
race announcer over a loudspeaker as Mater accelerated.

Lightning drove alongside Mater. "You did it, buddy! You can back off now!"

But Mater wasn't listening—he was having too much fun! He hollered,
"I AM SPEED!" Then he fired his jet engines.

"Four hundred sixty-five miles per hour!" said the race announcer.
"Six hundred forty miles per hour!"

Mater was giddy with excitement, and he couldn't stop laughing. This was amazing!

But as he went even faster, his body began to shake, and parts started to fall off. He felt himself losing control. Mater's wheels left the ground as he was moments away from crashing! Then everything went . . .

. . . peaceful, and Mater suddenly found himself floating in the sky among the clouds. Next to him was an elegant roadster, flapping her wings.

"The racers call me the Speed Demon," she said. "Mater, what are you doin' out here?"

"I was just scratchin' an itch," Mater said. "Thinkin', why can't I be the fastest?"

The Speed Demon listened and then said, "So, shall we be going?"

This was it. If Mater went with the Speed Demon, he would never get to see Lightning or his other friends again! Mater had to think fast.

"Close your eyes," Mater said. "How many tires am I holdin' up?"

While the Speed Demon thought of a number, Mater made his way back to his body.

"S'pose I can let one slip through the cracks," the Speed Demon said when she realized Mater had gotten away.

Mater completed his speed run and reunited with a very relieved Lightning. Noriyuki and the other crew chiefs were waiting back at the speed racer camp.

Noriyuki shouted, "Records have been shattered! This is just the beginning! We'll make history!"

But Mater didn't want to break any more speed records. He was just happy to be back with his best friend.

"Race you to the next town?" Lightning asked Mater.

"Go!" Mater replied, and the two cars took off for the highway.

After a long day on the road, Lightning and Mater decided to stop for the night and set up camp. Lightning got to work on a campfire while Mater befriended a camper, a Land Rover, and a station wagon.

"We hunt cryptids," said the Land Rover.

Lightning had no idea what he was talking about.

"Creatures on the fringes of our perception," said Mater.

"These woods are a hotbed for cryptid activity," the Land Rover said. "Specifically Big Foot."

Lightning thought it all sounded ridiculous
and just wanted to go to sleep. But Mater
told the cryptid hunters that he and Lightning
would accompany them on their Big Foot hunt.

Soon they were all outfitted with lights, cameras, and night-vision
goggles. Lightning noticed that for cars who were trying to hunt
something, they sure were making a lot of noise.

"Big Foot? Gimme a break," Lightning said, chuckling to himself. Then he heard a loud CRASH, and gasped as a huge shape appeared! Startled, Lightning took off, but the shape was quick and graceful and soon got ahead of him.

Lightning poured on the speed—and smacked right into a log, knocking himself out.

Lightning woke up only to find himself hanging inside a log cabin.

"You're awake?" Big Foot asked.

"Wait—you're not a monster," said Lightning. "You're a **monster truck**!"

"My name is Ivy, and I used to be a monster truck." Ivy explained that she'd gotten tired of smashing cars for a living, so she'd moved to the woods.

Suddenly, Mater burst through the door and said, "Gotcha, Big Foot!"

Ivy promptly hung him up right next to Lightning.

Lightning and Mater promised Ivy that if she cut them down, they'd help her stop the cryptid hunters from bothering her. She agreed, and they all went to her basement to come up with a plan.

"I'm stumped," Ivy said. "I keep scaring them off, but they just keep coming back."

Then she looked over at Mater, who was tangled up in some dryer hoses. That gave her an idea—a scary idea!

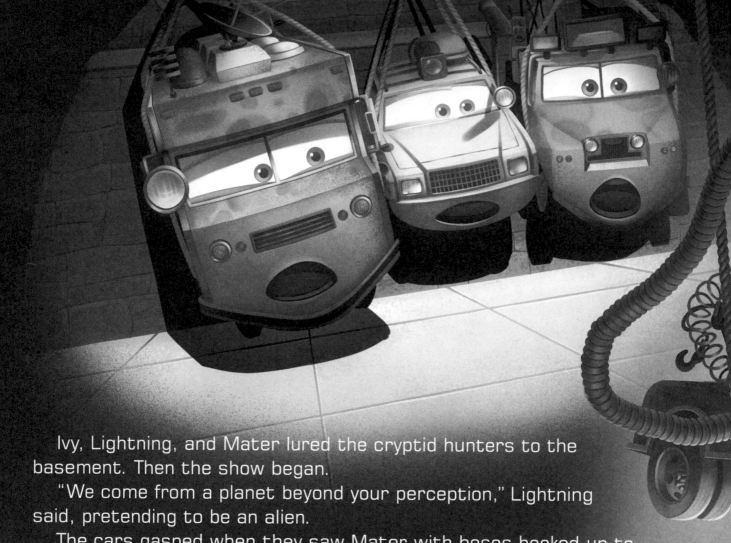

Ivy, Lightning, and Mater lured the cryptid hunters to the basement. Then the show began.

"We come from a planet beyond your perception," Lightning said, pretending to be an alien.

The cars gasped when they saw Mater with hoses hooked up to him. "Help me!" Mater cried.

Then Ivy, dressed up like a queen alien, confronted them. "Submit, foolish Earth-dwellers, so that we may drain the living essence from your husks!" She cut the line suspending the cars. Once they were free, the cryptid hunters ran screaming into the forest.

"It worked!" Ivy said with a big smile.

As the sun came up, Lightning said to Ivy, "You got your mountain back."

"Thanks for all your help. It was really fun to put on a performance again," Ivy replied. "So where are you guys headed?"

Lightning and Mater smiled at each other. They invited her to join them on their road trip! The three friends were soon cruising down the highway together, excited to see where the road would take them next.

SHOW TIME

Lightning and Mater were having a blast on their cross-country road trip. And their new friend Ivy was tagging along for the adventure. As they were driving down the highway, they spotted big tents in the distance.

"Oh, geez, it's a circus," Lightning said with an unhappy chuckle. Ivy gasped with delight and headed straight for the tents with her friends in tow.

Clown cars immediately came out to perform for them. Everyone found them amusing—except Lightning. He was terrified of clowns!

Mater and Lightning joined Ivy in the bleachers. The lights came up and a pair of ringmasters took the stage.

"Rare patrons," said one of the ringmasters. "Witness the dazzling spectacle that is . . . Circus Velocitas!"

BOOM! A cannon launched a clown car into the air. Stunt drivers zoomed up ramps, and others did loop-de-loops. There were even strongman forklifts who juggled cars!

Mater and Ivy thought the circus was incredible, but Lightning was too creeped out to enjoy any of it.

For the grand finale, the ringmasters called for a volunteer.
Lightning was thankful when the clown cars chose Ivy.
   Ivy approached the ringmasters and said, "I've got an idea,
if you don't mind. . . ."
   Moments later, she drove to the top of a ramp. Below,
all the clown cars were lined up.
      "Oh, no!" said Lightning. "What is she doing?"
      Ivy launched into the air and fell toward the clown
   cars like she was going to squash them! But instead,
   Ivy landed on one tire and danced between the
         cars without touching a single one!

Mater and Lightning couldn't believe what they were seeing. Ivy's dance was spectacular! She flipped and bounced into one of the rings. Then she spun around and jumped onto a strongman forklift, who lifted her into the air as she did a perfect pirouette. Everyone cheered! They were in awe of Ivy's performance.

"Ivy, you were amazing!" said Lightning.

"Guess what?" said Ivy. "They asked me to stay!"

Lightning was surprised that she had agreed, but he was happy that she had found a new home. "Well, maybe we'll meet again," he said.

"I really hope so," Ivy replied.

As Lightning and Mater headed back to the road, they said goodbye to their circus friends. In the distance, Ivy was already rehearsing and having the time of her life.

Lightning and Mater's adventures on the road continue. . . .